ZOMBIE SURF COMMANDOS FROM MARS!

There are more books about

THE WEIRD ZONE

#1 Zombie Surf Commandos From Mars!

#2 The Incredible Shrinking Kid!

coming to a bookstore near you . . .
#3 The Beast From Beneath the Cafeteria!

Stop!
Before you turn the page —
Take a piece of paper.
Pick up your pencil.
Draw a big triangle.

At the top point of the triangle write **Secret Government UFO Test Base**. At the left point write **Dinosaur Graveyard**. At the right point, **Humongous Horror Movie Studios**. And in the exact center of the triangle write Grover's Mill.

Ah, Grover's Mill. A perfectly normal town, bustling with shops, gas stations, motels, restaurants, and schools. A small town with a great big heart, nestled snugly in the midst of —

Wait! Did we say normal? A studio where they film the cheapest horror movies ever made? The world's largest and smelliest graveyard of ancient dinosaur bones? A secret army base filled with captured alien spacecraft?

All this makes poor Grover's Mill the exact center of supreme intergalactic weirdness!

Turn the page.
If you dare.
Enter The Weird Zone!

THE WEIRD ZONE

ZOMBIE SURF
COMMANDOS
FROM MARS!

by Tony Abbott

illustrated by Broeck Steadman

A
LITTLE APPLE
PAPERBACK

SCHOLASTIC INC.
New York Toronto London Auckland Sydney

ISBN 0-590-67433-1

12 11 10 9 8 7 6 5   6 7 8 9/9 0 1/0

Printed in the U.S.A   40
First Scholastic printing, July 1996

To George Nicholson,
a valiant friend,
for making this so much fun

Contents

ZOMBIE SURF COMMANDOS FROM MARS!

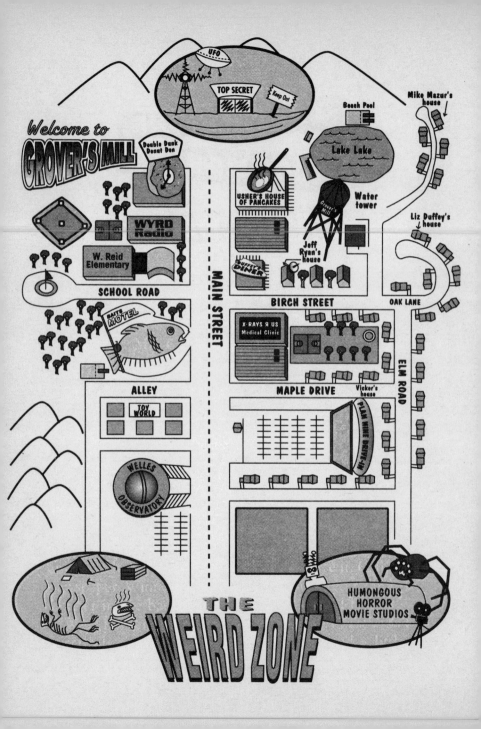

A Different Kind of Town

The summer sun rose slowly over the town of Grover's Mill. Liz Duffey stepped into the shadow of a giant glazed donut and waited for her two friends.

Bong! The thirty-foot pastry clock sitting atop the Double Dunk Donut Den chimed the hour.

"Ah," Liz sighed to herself. "Another day in —"

Sssss! A stream of smoke rose in the sky.

"— The Weird Zone!"

Liz gazed over at the giant pancake pan perched on the roof of Usher's House of Pancakes, otherwise known as U-HOP.

The pancake pan hissed the hour, every hour on the hour.

Yes, thought Liz, the place was pretty weird. But the people were even weirder. She had a name for them, too: *Zoners*. Just about everybody who lived in Grover's Mill was a Zoner — except her, of course. And her friends.

Well, most of them.

"Hmmm," she mumbled to herself. "Ten A.M. I wonder how long it'll be before the first really weird thing happens."

"Spit on Mars!" a voice cried out.

"No," Liz suddenly snapped back. "Spitting is disgusting. Besides, Mars is way too far. Wait, who said that?"

"I did!" said the voice.

Liz whirled around to see a quivering newspaper with legs. She pulled the paper down.

Behind it was the face of Jeff Ryan, normally round and smiling. But now his expression was one of total shock. *"Spit on*

Mars," he repeated. "What . . . what could it mean?"

Liz bit her lip and glared at the boy. She'd known Jeff since they were in first grade together. He was best friends with her best friend's brother. He was okay, she thought, but . . . well, Jeff was in real danger of becoming a Zoner!

He stood there, brushing back the zip haircut spiking up from his forehead. He silently mouthed the words he was reading. His forehead got more and more wrinkled.

Liz took pity on him. "You know, Jeff, they always spell everything wrong in the *Grover's Mill Gazette*. Read to me and I will translate."

Jeff brightened and began. "Exports at the Wells Lavatory discoed around stringy spit on the sour face of Mars a few dogs ago." He looked at Liz.

She thought for a second. "Experts at the Welles Observatory discovered a strange spot on the surface of Mars a few days ago?"

Jeff nodded. "Ah, a spot on Mars." He read some more. "No one can seem to explain it."

"I can explain it, Jeff," said Liz. "It's The Weird Zone. It's Double Dunk Weirdness Time." She pointed over at the Baits Motel, a huge fish-shaped building across from Dr. Orloff's X-Rays Я Us Medical Clinic. "I mean, the whole place ought to be called Weirdo's Mill!"

The two kids began to walk up Main Street toward the beach.

"So you think it's strange?" asked Jeff.

Liz sighed. "Listen, Jeff, the first step in battling The Zone is seeing the weirdness. If you don't, you could become one of them!" She narrowed her eyes and scanned the people on the street. "Zoners!" she hissed. "Ugh!"

Jeff followed her stare. He ran his hand over his zip cut. "But aren't other towns pretty much like ours?"

4

"I hope not!" Liz gasped, her eyes glazing over like that big donut. "But if I ever get away, I'll let you know."

Jeff nodded. "Sean Vickers has been away for almost the whole summer. When he comes back, maybe he can tell us what it's like. Hey, when *is* he coming back, anyway?"

"Never, if I can help it!" called a voice from behind both of them. They turned to see a girl in a W. Reid Elementary T-shirt and pink sunglasses. She had a beach towel tucked under her arm.

It was Holly Vickers, Liz's best friend since kindergarten. They did everything together.

Holly smiled really big at both of them. "My goofy brother Sean is at some goofy camp. I think it's called Camp Goofy."

Liz laughed. Holly always made her laugh.

"Hey, wait a second," said Jeff. "Sean's okay. In fact, I think he's pretty great."

"Yeah, I think he's great, too," said Holly.

"Especially when he's at camp!"

Liz laughed again as Holly pushed up her funny glasses and winked. "Come on, guys," Liz said finally. "Let's hit the lake before it dries up."

Jeff smiled at both of them. "I've got a feeling that today is going to be very fun."

Liz wondered whether to tell Jeff that it only *might* be very fun, but it would *definitely* be very strange. "Just keep your eyes open for the next weird thing to happen."

Then, as if to say — here I am! — the next weird thing did happen.

As the kids passed an alley on their way to the beach — a ten-foot-tall green slimy blob of gunk slid out and oozed toward them!

Thick red liquid was dripping from its teeth.

Yes! The blob of gunk had teeth! And two enormous black eyeballs glaring down at the kids. Yes! It had eyeballs!

Liz grabbed Jeff by his shirt and pulled

him out of the way, but Holly was too far ahead. "Holly!" she cried out. "Run!"

Too late!

The oozy blob had her in its — its — ooze!

Say, Ooze That Blob, Anyway?

Holly flung her arms wildly! She cried out!

She tried to pull away, but the thing wouldn't let her go!

It was horrible. It was disgusting. In a matter of seconds, Holly was totally swallowed up by the creature.

She screamed out a feeble last word — "Dad!"

Dad? It was then that Liz saw a man's tiny head pop out of the slimy green mass.

"Dad!" Holly repeated, jumping up to the head and kissing its cheek. A moment later — *kkrripp!* — the sound of Velcro, and out popped Todd Vickers, the not-at-all-famous movie director, writer, producer, special effects person, camera person, and in fact the *only* person at nearby Humongous Horror Movie Studios.

"Howdy, slime fans!" Mr. Vickers said with a big smile. He patted the oozy costume next to him, then wiped his hand on his pants.

"Meet the star of my latest film. Do you love him, or what?" Mr. Vickers pointed down the street to the sign over the ticket booth at Plan Nine Drive-in. Bloodred letters spelled out — *Blobbo, the Hideous Mutant Brainoid!*

Liz nodded. Every time she went to the Drive-in and saw the screen flash with the words *Another Humongous Horror!* she knew that it was going to: (a) be a horror movie about something creepy, (b) be filmed in Grover's Mill in less than a week, (c) have lousy acting and a dumb plot, and (d) have special effects that weren't all that special.

"Cool!" Jeff gasped. He looked over the

quivering lump of ooze. "But what's the difference between a brain and a brainoid?"

Mr. Vickers stroked his chin. "I don't know . . . what?"

Jeff frowned. "I was asking you . . ."

"Oh, never mind that," Mr. Vickers went on, quickly hiding the brainoid costume under a large black cloth. "Tonight, at the very stroke of eight o'clock, this very night, yes, tonight, just before the movie starts, Blobbo and I are going to give the audience such a total gross-out, skin-crawling scare. Everyone will wish they'd all bought popcorn!"

"Popcorn?" asked Jeff. "Why?"

"For the bags!" Mr. Vickers chuckled loudly.

"Huh?" Liz said.

"To be sick in!" Mr. Vickers laughed again, a little less loudly.

"Dad!" cried Holly. "I have friends here!"

It was true that sometimes Mr. Vickers seemed to forget he was a grown-up.

"Anyway," he continued, "we're going to

fire up the floodlights again. People will pour in from miles away!" He pointed at two floodlights standing like cannons in front of the Drive-in.

Liz remembered last week's movie opening. The night sky had been white with crisscrossing spotlights. They were supposed to attract people from out of town, but it never really worked.

No one came to Grover's Mill unless it was by mistake. But Mr. Vickers always had hope.

"Be there tonight at eight P.M. sharp. You'll be thrilled! You'll be chilled! Hmm. Speaking of chilled, I'd better keep Pudding Boy on ice till tonight." Mr. Vickers smiled and hugged Holly. Then he pushed the blubbery blob up the street.

"The lake is calling us!" Liz pleaded.

A moment later, the hot sidewalk came to an end. The three friends were at the beach.

To the right was an old shingled beach clubhouse, with a multicolored awning and party lights. To the left was a hot dog stand. Straight ahead was the lake.

Young and old alike were lying on the sand or frolicking happily in the water.

"Ah!" Liz gasped as she took in the scene before her. "Behold the splendor of Lake Lake, chums. Notice the wide sweep of sandy beach, washed by the gentle sudsy lap-lap-lap of surf. Gosh, it's beautiful!"

The giant O of water, surrounded by sand, just sat there like warm milk at the bottom of a cereal bowl.

Holly gave Liz a look, unrolled her towel, and plopped down in the sand. "Lake *Lake*? I always thought that was a strange name. Did somebody run out of ideas?"

"No," said Liz, taking a step toward the water. "The lake was named after an old man called Lake."

Jeff nodded. "Cool. What was his first name?"

Liz shrugged. "Old man." She watched a few teenagers paddle out on surfboards to the calm center of Lake Lake. Surf's down, she thought.

Farther up the beach another bunch of teenagers was having a cookout. One of them was tapping on a set of bongo drums and groaning a teenage song about kissing and love and stuff.

Liz curled her lip and rolled her eyes. "Yuck."

"Anybody want a hot dog?" asked Jeff.

"For breakfast?" said Holly.

Both girls shook their heads, so Jeff ran off to the hot dog stand. In a few moments he was back, holding something dripping with gobs of mustard.

Liz leaned back on her towel and closed her eyes. Her nose wrinkled suddenly like a worm when you touch it. She opened her eyes. "What's that gross smell?"

Jeff sniffed his hot dog and shook his head. "Not me."

"It's him!" Holly gasped, pointing. "He's wearing socks with his sandals! Black ones! Eew!"

Liz stood up and gazed across the sand to see waves of heat rising up from the feet of Mr. Bell, principal of W. Reid Elementary School.

The tall bathing-trunked figure of Principal Bell, so terrifying during the school year, seemed out of place on the sunny beach at Lake Lake.

Holly stood next to Liz and watched Principal Bell walk slowly up to the beach clubhouse. He went into the public rest room.

"Zoner," whispered Liz. Holly nodded.

But something else was happening, too.

The teenagers who had paddled out on surfboards suddenly came running back from the water. Their faces were pale. They waved their arms.

"Strangers stole our boards!" one of them cried out, pointing toward the very center of Lake Lake.

The lake was rumbling and bubbling up from the depths like water boiling for spaghetti.

Suddenly, the lake's surface broke in a rush of smoky air. It wafted into Liz's nostrils. "Pee-yew!" she cried, backing up. "*That's* the smell!"

But that wasn't the worst part.

When the bubbles broke, the water immediately erupted into a tall wave, frothy white on top and deep blue-black in the middle.

But even *that* wasn't the worst part.

The huge wave built up and up and began to fall, thundering forward from the middle of the lake and heading right for shore!

But even *THAT* wasn't the worst part.

What Liz saw next struck ultimate terror in her heart.

"*Ahhhhhhhhh!*" she screamed.

Surf's Up!

Coming out from the crest of the giant wave were the tips of the teenagers' surfboards. Each board was jammed with five or six figures.

Boy, were they good surfers! They nosed under the crest, swaying back and forth on the boards like experts!

"What —!" cried Holly.

"Whoa —!" cried Jeff.

"Weird —!" cried Liz.

These surfers were not normal everyday teenage surfers. They had even worse skin problems! Their faces were horrible and gray. They had bald scalps with stringy wisps of white hair flying back in the breeze and ears that drooped and sagged to their shoulders. And their foreheads bulged.

Some had big gaping holes instead of noses!

Everyone who saw them screamed and bolted from the water.

"Out of towners!" one person screeched.

"Strangers at our lake!" cried another.

"Those dudes stole our boards!" a teen boy complained.

Kkkkerrrwooooshhhh! The wave crashed on the sandy shore, and the horrible gray creatures leaped off the surfboards onto the sand.

Jeff stared at them, dropping his hot dog in the sand. Mustard side down. "Ooops, I guess I'll just have to get another one!" He shot up a dune and dived over the counter of the hot dog stand.

In a flash, everyone was screaming and running all over the beach. People were bumping into each other in a mad scramble to leave.

But Liz couldn't move. She stared at the bulging heads, black eyes rolling around and around, purple tongues hanging out of lipless mouths, and large holes for noses. "No, these are definitely not regular surfers," she mumbled. "Teenagers, either!"

"Run and hide!" cried Holly, grabbing Liz.

"Right!" said Liz. She tore off with Holly and jumped over the counter of the hot dog stand, landing on Jeff.

"No fair!" he grunted. "I got here first!"

"You took the best place!" Holly snapped.

The kids poked their heads over the counter.

The gray creatures shuffled up the beach. They wore brightly colored suits with big, flared shoulders and army belts crisscrossing their chests.

"Different," said Jeff. "But stylish!"

The creatures shuffled their feet, which glinted from their shiny silver boots.

"They should pick up their feet," Holly snarled softly. "My mom would kill them for spraying sand like that!"

"From the looks of these guys," said Liz, "I'd say someone beat your mom to it."

"Nice lake," Jeff hissed. "Who knew dead people lived here?"

Suddenly, horror struck Liz. A brightly colored beach ball rolled over a dune right to the silver-booted feet of one very ugly creature.

He made a gurgling, whining sort of noise.

"No!" gasped Liz. "Look!"

A little girl, no more than a year old, came stumbling up to the top of the dune after the beach ball. A few steps behind her was her father. "Say Da-da," he coaxed her. "Come on, honey, say Da-da. Say your first word!"

The toddler giggled and scrambled to the top of the dune. She stopped. Inches from her face was the hideously ugly, dusty, dead-looking face of the creature. It towered over her.

The thing's forehead breathed in and out. He gurgled and groaned down at the tiny girl.

She wobbled, her chubby fingers waving in the air at the thing standing before her. Suddenly, she spoke.

"Z-z-z-zom — beeeee!" she mumbled.

Her first word.

Liz heard the creature whine a little, and tilt its head to the side. Then it lunged at the little girl.

"Hey!" screamed the girl's father, yanking her back down the dune. "I thought this was a private lake!"

Jeff tapped Liz on the shoulder. "Did that girl say *zombie*?"

The flaky creature grunted and gurgled and whined some more, then snapped up the beach ball. He held it out in one hand, made his other into a fist, and served the ball high into the air.

Within seconds, he and his fellow zombies were playing a heated game of beach volleyball.

"Is this weird or is this weird?" asked Holly.

Liz nodded slowly. "Both."

At one point, an ugly creature leaped for the ball, missed, and fell flat in the sand.

Kra — thump! The creature shattered into a dozen parts — hands, arms, legs, feet, head — all went scattering across the sand.

"I'm gonna be sick!" Holly gulped.

In a flash, however, another creature picked up the detached head and spiked it over the net.

"Point!" groaned the zombies.

Brain Eaters!

"Oh," gasped Holly, cupping her hand over her mouth. "That's just gross!"

"Right," whispered Liz. Then, taking herself by surprise, she added, "But a good lesson in team spirit."

Something told her she was right about that. Team spirit. Principal Bell always talked about it.

"Excuse me," said Jeff, "but unless we plan on being zombie food, we've got to get out of here!"

He looked around. "Maybe we can bolt for the clubhouse while they're playing head ball."

Suddenly, the creatures stopped playing.

"Or maybe not," Jeff said.

The creatures shuffled around the cook-out fire that the teenagers had left burning. They splashed water on it using an abandoned beach pail. A thick puff of smoke filled the air. They sat down and breathed the smoke in.

Their dead eyes bulged.

One of them stood up. He was taller than the rest. His head had pulsing knobs all over it and his Ping-Pong eyeballs rolled from side to side.

"Good-looking guy," Liz whispered. "He must be their leader."

Another creature picked up the set of bongo drums the teenagers had left behind and began tapping on them slowly, rhythmically.

Tap-tappa-tap. Tap-tappa-tap.

The tall one moved to the center of the group and started swaying back and forth to the beat. All the bulging Ping-Pong eye-

balls looked to him. He began to sing. The
song went like this —

> Once, we were so cool and shiny,
> Now we are dead and we're whiny.
> Hey! We've all gone so flaky
> And now our poor hearts are achy.
>> To get to our planet so far —
>> The planet that we call Mar —
>> zzzzzzzzzzzzzzzzzzzzzzzzzz!

"Mar — *zzzzzzzzzzz?*" Jeff snorted into
Liz's shoulder. "That doesn't make sense."

"They're dead, Jeff," said Liz. But before
she could brush her shoulder, all the creatures rose to sing a second verse!

> Our skin is dry like crepe paper,
> If we don't eat brains — we're vapor!
> Fresh brains are good for what ails us,
> Until the mother ship sails us
>> Back to our planet so far —
>> The planet that we call Mar —
>> zzzzzzzzzzzzzzzzzzzzzzzzzzzz!

28

At that instant, the knob-faced creature pointed up to the sky directly over the mountains to the north. All the zombies looked.

"Mars is that way," mumbled Liz. "These zombies are from Mars!"

A tear rolled from one of knob-head's eyeballs and disappeared in the flaky skin of his cheek.

"And they're homesick," Holly whispered. "That's so sad. I wonder if they need help or — "

"We need brains!" the zombie leader shouted loudly. "Living, breathing brains! Or else we will all dry out and die. When you see a good brain, put a little mark on their forehead, like this!" He tapped at the air. "It means — good eats for later!"

Then the bongo pounding started again. This time it was faster, harder, and more violent than before. The groaning and droning and moaning got louder. The creatures stomped around in the sand. Some of them began to wail like wolves.

"I think maybe they're hungry," Holly whispered.

"Yeah, hungry for brains!" Liz said.

"But still, one of them was crying," said Holly.

"Um," Jeff mumbled. "All in favor of getting out of here say so now!"

"So now!" said Liz.

"So now!" said Holly.

The alien zombie drumming on the bongos was going crazy, pounding harder and harder!

Kra — THUMP!

A flaky gray finger smashed against the bongos, snapped off, flipped over, and landed on the hot dog counter inches away from the kids!

Liz moved back instantly. The finger wriggled across the counter.

Then, before you could say — *gross!* — it sprang up and tapped Holly right in the forehead!

"Grosssssss!" she screamed, jumping up.

The bongos stopped. The creatures turned toward the hot dog stand.

"Brains!" The knob-faced one howled, pointing at the kids.

Snaaaaack Time!

Immediately, the surfers from Mars split into two attack groups and charged the hot dog stand.

"Uh-oh," Jeff gasped. "Commandos!"

"Sorry, guys!" cried Holly, rubbing her forehead. "The finger grossed me out."

"Never mind!" yelled Liz, grabbing a handful of uncooked dogs and stacking them on the counter in front of her. "Grab some ammo!" Then Liz began hurling the hot dogs one by one over the counter at the zombies. "We have to defend ourselves!"

The zombies leaped and jumped at the hot dogs. They gobbled them right up and kept charging.

"They're hungry, all right," quipped Jeff. "Now they need the good stuff!" He reached over and pulled up two squeeze bottles of thick, yellow mustard. He laid them down on the counter like little cannons and began pounding them with his fists.

Splurp! Sklish! Splap!

Spurts and splashes of mustard shot through the air and into the faces of the zombie attackers. They dived for the sand to avoid the spicy spray.

"Ugh!" groaned one zombie, flicking his flaky finger at a fleck of mustard in his dead eye!

"Ha!" yelped Jeff. "A real snack attack!"

Liz wondered how long they could keep this up. "Feed me! Feed me!" she cried, hurling hot dog after hot dog at the zombie commandos.

"They'll remember this as Custer's last hot dog stand!" Jeff yelped, pounding more.

The zombies leaped for the dogs and gobbled them. "Not brains," knob-face said, a hot dog in each hand. "But not bad!"

"Out of dogs!" screamed Holly. "We'll have to switch to burgers!" She tore open a bag of hamburger patties and began flinging them wildly like Frisbees.

Suddenly, the zombies stopped their attack to watch the burgers zipping overhead. The patties looked like little flying saucers spinning across the blue desert sky.

"Home!" cried one zombie. A tear welled up and disappeared into its flaky cheek.

"Oh!" gasped Holly. "That's so sweet!"

"Brains!" knob-face reminded his fellow attackers.

"Brainnnnnns!" the commandos chanted.

Suddenly — *craaaaaaack!*

An arm broke through the back of the stand!

"They're getting in!" Liz cried out, ducking back as a gray hand groped around.

"I just splurped my last splurp!" Jeff gasped, pounding a tiny drip of mustard

from an empty squeeze bottle.

"Get the brains!" the knobby zombie leader shouted to his troops.

In a flash, Liz bolted over the front of the counter, pulling Holly along with her. They dropped to the sand. "To the clubhouse!" Liz cried. Then she and Holly began to make their way across the dunes to the old shingled building.

Jeff tumbled out of the stand right behind them, but he slipped getting to his feet.

"Help!" he shouted. But the Martians cut him off. He looked around the dunes. There was nowhere to go. Nowhere but up!

Jeff bolted to his feet and climbed up a lifeguard chair looming above him.

But the ugly squad attacked the chair!

Flaky gray hands clutched at Jeff's feet. He kicked back, stomping his heels wildly. *Kkkk!* A flaky head snapped back and dropped to the sand!

"Sorry, man!" winced Jeff.

Suddenly, from behind him, he heard a call.

"Hey, zombies! Nyah-nyah!"

The zombies turned.

It was Liz, holding up her bangs and showing her forehead. Holly was behind her, making a face at Liz.

"Yum!" yelled knob-face. "Let's go!"

The squad deserted Jeff on the chair and shuffled across the sand after Liz.

"Hey!" shouted Jeff. "What's wrong with *my* brain?"

THONKA-THONKA-THONKA!

A huge roaring, grinding, thundering sound filled the air. The sky darkened above the beach. The water in Lake Lake swirled.

Liz gasped as a black shadow spread low across the sand.

Holly fell instantly to the sand.

Liz dived. "Watch out!" she screamed.

R*RRRRRR!* It was horrible! The beach turned into a swirling tornado of wind.

Liz and Holly lay motionless on the sand.

Jeff didn't. He started walking into the tornado. "Mother?" he cried.

"Jeff, no!" Liz screamed. But the dark, thundering noise came so low she couldn't move.

Out of the noise and wind a jet-powered helicopter appeared. It roared low over the beach. Sand swirled up in funnels everywhere.

Then, a woman's face smiled from the

front bubble window of the helicopter. She waved.

Jeff waved back. "Hi, Mom!"

An instant later, the helicopter roared away.

Liz peered around. "Hey! The zombies are gone!" It was true. Not a gray skin flake in sight!

Holly jumped up. "Your *mom*? That was your mom? Does she always scare people to death?"

Jeff looked hurt. "Well, yeah. People always drop down and play dead when she goes over. Just like you did. Anyway, she scared the zombies away."

Liz glared at Jeff. With a mother like that, she wondered if it was already too late to help him.

Jeff frowned. "What's the big deal? It's just my mom."

"Okay, Jeff," Liz said. "I thought you told us your mother worked in a shoe store. What does she really do?"

Jeff shrugged. "She works in a shoe store."

"Wrong!" said Liz, like a game show host.

"She sells seashells by the sea — " Jeff started to say.

"Jeff!" Liz snapped.

"Oh, man! What can I say?" he said. "She won't tell me what she does. It's a secret. She and my dad are really quiet about it all."

"Helicopters aren't quiet," said Holly, scanning the beach for anything that moved.

"Yeah," Jeff admitted, looking at the black dot disappearing over the hills. "That's a little strange. A chopper flies to my house every morning, drops a rope ladder, and my mom climbs up and goes to work. Every night at eight it flies back and she parachutes down."

Liz turned Jeff around by his shoulders and pointed to the far hills. "Your mom works just over that giant pancake pan, in those hills, in a secret government test base, doesn't she?"

Jeff bit his lower lip and looked down at the sand. "Well, one night, I heard her say something to my dad, but it doesn't make sense."

"What did she say?" asked Liz.

"Yeah," said Holly. "You can tell us."

"Fly sauce," Jeff said. "She works with fly sauce."

Holly wrinkled her face up. "Fly sauce? Why would she work with fly sauce? I mean, what *is* fly sauce?"

Liz jumped up. "No!" she exclaimed. "Not fly sauce. Flying saucers! I knew it!"

Jeff's mouth nearly dropped to his chest. "Flying saucers? Really?

"Listen, you guys," Liz went on. "I always knew Grover's Mill was weird, and this proves it. We must be in like the world center of UFO landings and stuff. This place is a magnet for weirdness from every corner of the universe."

"From Mar — zzzz?" Jeff looked thoughtful. "That might explain these dead guys with the — "

Tap! Tap! Tap! The sound of bongos suddenly broke through the air.

Liz felt cold fear swat her back. A shiver fell across her shoulders. Her spine felt like cold jelly was sliding down it.

Holly jerked around and pointed to a nearby dune. "Maybe they're dead — but they're back!"

"Braaaaains!" the zombie knob-faced leader whined, as a squad of Martian commando surf zombies piled over a dune and charged at the three kids!

But the sand slowed the zombies down! Good thing the undead were wearing thick-soled, silver space boots!

"To the clubhouse, quick," Liz shouted. In a flash the kids tore across the sand and leaped up to the wooden porch.

Pretty party lights swung all along the canvas awning. Liz stepped into the building.

Suddenly, she screeched to a stop and

shot her finger up to her lips. Holly stopped and rubbed her forehead where the finger had touched her. "I feel — *grumpfff*."

Jeff put his hand over her mouth. "Shhh."

"Ohhh!" A low groaning sound came from inside the beach house. Then, the shuffling of feet.

"It's them!" hissed Jeff. "They're already in the beach house! We're surrounded by an army of undead living zombie corpses!"

An instant later — *flam!* — a white door flashed open in front of the kids.

Liz's heart froze.

The Mark of the Zombie!

A tall figure appeared in the shadowy doorway. It breathed out loud. "Hmmm?"

"Principal Bell!" shouted Liz, recognizing the man stepping out of the public rest room.

"Yes, Miss Duffey!" the tall man boomed, shuffling out under the party lights. "And what are you young students doing at the *beach*, hmm? There are only a few more weeks in my summer reading program! Where, oh where, are your stacks of books?"

"Um, Mr. Bell," said Holly, rubbing her forehead. "Out there . . . on the sand . . . we saw . . ."

"Yes?" he said, peering down toward the beach. "That's not the way to the library."

"Zombies!" Liz burst out. "Flaky, ugly skin!"

Principal Bell's eyebrows shot up, then he smiled. "Ho-ho! You must mean Miss Krafnutter, bless her soul. One hundred and four years old and every minute spent in the sun!"

"No!" insisted Liz, her voice trembling. "Zombies. Attack zombies. Commandos!"

"From Mars!" Jeff cried.

"They surf, too," Holly added.

Principal Bell stepped off the porch and walked out onto the sand. He peered first one way then another. Liz followed his gaze. The beach was deserted. No army of undead living zombie corpses. Not a single one!

"Wait a second — " Liz started.

"Tut-tut," boomed the principal, frowning a terrible frown upon the children. "Year-round school. That's what you youngsters need. Builds team spirit! Now,

off with you, or I'll call your parents. Shoo!"

He strode away over the nearest dune, a little white slip of bathroom tissue trailing behind one of his socked and sandaled feet.

An instant later, the beach was empty as far as the eye could see. Totally deserted.

"Guys, we've got to warn people about the zombies," said Liz, finally letting out a breath.

"Wait," Holly whined. She rubbed her forehead some more. "Is there a dot?" She pushed her forehead out for Liz and Jeff to look at.

Liz stared closely at the dark, flaky smudge above Holly's left eyebrow. She didn't like the look of it at all. But her best friend seemed scared. "Just a little dot, Holly." She nudged Jeff.

"Right," said Jeff, nodding really big and backing away. "Not much at all."

Holly rubbed her head harder. "I feel weird."

"Well, you're in the right place for it," said Liz, scanning the quiet beach. "Let's get going."

"But what if we're too late?" asked Jeff. "What if zombies have already snacked on the town?"

"Only one way to find out," said Liz. She ran through the clubhouse and out the front door.

They only stopped when they reached Main Street. People were walking around as if they didn't know alien zombies were after their brains. The Double Dunk Donut Den clock said nearly noon.

"Looks normal," said Jeff.

"Maybe we just imagined it all?" Holly said quietly, trying to smile. "Maybe it'll all be okay."

Liz shook her head. "Sure, and I'm Glinda, the good witch. Those zombies are here, all right. They're in the alleys and back streets. They're in the shadows and around the corners. They're with us!"

Jeff looked in every direction. "You're

being spooky, Liz. I don't like it when you're spooky."

She stepped slowly down the street. Jeff followed closely behind her. Holly was last.

"These weird dudes came out of the lake, right?" Liz said. "But how did they get there? They look yucky, like zombies, but they're not everyday regular zombies. They're — "

"From Mars!" Holly cut in. "And it's the air here that makes their skin all flaky and dead!"

Liz stopped and turned to her best friend with the dot on her head. "How do you know that?"

Holly wrinkled her forehead. "I don't know, I just do."

"Maybe that's why they need brains to survive," Jeff said. "Because of the air. *Fresh brains are good for what ails us.* They sang that, right?"

"And they put a dot on us," Holly began

to whine, "when they want to eat our kid brains."

"Just a little dot," said Liz, nudging Jeff again.

"Not much at all," Jeff said.

"Home," said Holly. "I want to go home."

"Good idea," said Liz. "Maybe our parents can help!"

They ran without stopping until they reached Holly's house. Liz and Jeff followed Holly in.

Mrs. Vickers was in the kitchen, wearing a yellow apron and green oven mitts. The room smelled of cookies baking. "Dear, your face is dirty!" she gasped at Holly's smudged forehead.

"Zombies, Mom," Holly mumbled, yawning. "They want to eat my brain."

Mrs. Vickers frowned, turned down the oven, then removed her mitts. "You know what your father always says — *a brain is a terrible thing to taste*. Oh! Such a funny man!"

Holly nodded. "I'm really sleepy. Can I take a nap?" That was it. Holly shuffled from the kitchen down a hall to her room. She closed her door.

Mrs. Vickers turned and smiled. "Oh, well. Cookies anyone?"

Liz's brain began to buzz. "Um, no thanks, Mrs. Vickers." She pulled Jeff out the door to the Vickers' front yard. "Jeff, I think we need experts. Jeff?"

But Jeff just hunched over the sidewalk and stared at the cracks between his feet.

"Jeff? You okay?" Liz asked.

Suddenly, he slapped his cheeks. "What do they want?" he screamed. "Why are they here? Why us? What's going to happen?" He buried his head in his hands. "It doesn't make sense!"

Liz patted Jeff on the shoulder. She knew the feeling. She'd lived a lifetime trying to figure out why things didn't make sense.

She wondered for a second if Jeff would

really get it together when things got tough. She decided he would, but he'd need some help.

She took a breath, and she began to sing.

Hey, my friend, don't worry,
Life can sting sometimes.
Like juice gets in a hangnail,
When you squeeze ripe limes.
But if you take my haaaaaand
Life can be so graaaaaaaaand!

"Sorry," said Liz. "The zombies made me feel musical."

Jeff smiled a weak smile at her. "Thanks. It worked. I do feel better." He looked up at the silver radar dish spinning on his roof two streets away. "My dad's home. He'll help us. Come on!"

They took the corner of Maple and Elm at full speed, and ran for Jeff's house on Birch Street.

Liz looked around as she ran. In the distance, she saw the Plan Nine Drive-in. Mr. Vickers was moving the floodlights for tonight's big premiere.

An image flashed into her mind. Last week's opening night. Lights flooding the dark sky. To bring in out of towners to see the movie.

Something oozed in her mind. *Out of towners?* Maybe the lights *did* work. "Jeff. When did they find that spot on Mars?"

"A few dogs — I mean — a few days ago," Jeff said.

Clouds drifted across the giant July sun. A breeze swept in. Suddenly Liz's brain clicked.

"The Martians saw the lights! That's why they're here! And they surfed out of the lake — "

Before she could finish, she heard something.

Tap-tappa-tap. Tappa-tappa-tap.

Bongo drums.

Alone!

"Zombies!" screeched Liz. "Ruuunnnn!"

The kids shot off as if they had rockets on their feet. A second later the street behind them was filled with a groaning band of Martian zombies!

"OHHHHHHH!" the zombies moaned. Leading them was knob-face, the tall creature with the pulsing forehead. He gestured once and the Martians grunted and charged after the kids.

"Uh-oh!" yelled Jeff. "They're doing that commando thing again!"

Jeff and Liz tore off between two houses. All the while the zombies were gurgling really dumb words —

We don't ride planes,
We don't take trains,
We don't need canes,
We have no veins,
We just eat brains!
That's right, uh-huh,
We just eat braaaaaaains!

"Boy, where do they come up with those words?" Jeff huffed, running for a low hedge.

But Liz took a shortcut across the Sweeneys' front corner. Their sprinkler was on.

"Hey, you!" Mr. Sweeney cried from the door as Liz trampled the grass. "My lawn! My lawn!"

But she couldn't stop to explain. Not with zombies after her!

Suddenly, she slipped on the wet grass, and took a spill. Jeff leaped over the far hedge. Knob-face called out commands to the commandos and they split into two squads, one going after Jeff while the other shuffled after Liz.

"Run, Jeff!" Liz shouted as she tried to escape down Oak Lane. She ran panting to her front door, tumbled in, and slammed it behind her.

Still the zombies came. Liz leaped to a window. She saw knob-face motioning for his creatures to surround the entire house.

"Mom!" Liz screamed out. No answer.

She ran from room to room, shouting.

"Mom! Mom!"

No answer.

Of course! Her mother was at work. It was lunchtime. She owned a restaurant! Where else would she be? Outside, the horrible creatures began pounding on the windows.

"No!" Liz scrambled to the phone on the kitchen counter. The red light on the answering machine was blinking. Liz pressed the button.

Beep went the machine. "Hi, honey," began her mother's voice. "I'll be at the Diner all day today waiting for cold cuts. Hope you're having fun. Love you!" *Beep.*

Liz fumbled for the phone. She dialed the number. It began to ring.

Suddenly — *boom! Boom! Boom!* The zombies were hurling themselves at the doors.

"Mom!"

"Hi, dear," her mother answered. "Did you — "

"Mom!" Liz yelled into the phone. "Outside the house! The living dead. Gray, flaky skin — "

"Mrs. Krafnutter? Dear, she's very old."

"No, Mom!" Liz could hardly form the words.

Boom! Boom! The windows rattled. The front door shook on its hinges. They were getting in!

RRRRRR! came a loud sound from the phone.

"I'm sorry, dear," her mother inter-

rupted. "I can't hear you! The truck from Santa Mira just pulled up here. I have to go. See you in a bit!"

Nnnnnnnn. Her mother had hung up.

"No!" Liz cried out to the empty house. She threw the phone down and ran upstairs, tripping three times before finally reaching the landing.

CRASH! The sound of glass shattering!

"You won't get me!" she screeched, leaping for her bedroom door and slamming it behind her. She turned the bolt.

Suddenly — *KKKRREEUNNCH!*

The door blew off its hinges! Liz tumbled to the floor. A huge gray creature shuffled in!

Its skin was flaking off like ash on a burnt log. Its forehead bulged and breathed like a lung.

It smelled like something dead.

Flump! A piece of its cheek fell to the floor and shattered into dust.

It *was* something dead!

"Brains!" gurgled the horrible voice.

A flaky finger shot up at her forehead. Liz swooned. Her breakfast tumbled in her stomach and lurched up her throat.

The creature dived at her.

Everything went dark.

One of — Them!

*B*oom-boom-boom!

It sounded like the whole house was under attack. The front door was being pounded and knocked and kicked!

Liz felt herself trying to run away.

But something was holding her down! Something cold and lifeless. She felt it across her face.

She opened her eyes.

It was — a hand!

It was — her own hand!

She lay sprawled on her bedroom floor amid all the scraps of wood that were once the door.

Then she noticed the light coming from the window. It was different. The sun was nearly down. It was almost nighttime.

Boom-boom-boom!

"They're still after me!" Liz bolted to her feet, looking for somewhere to hide. Then she caught a glimpse of her face in the mirror on her wall. She stared into it, lifting her bangs off her forehead. "Please, no . . ." She held her breath.

No spot!

She breathed out again.

Boom-boom-boom!

"Liz! Liz! Open the door!" cried a voice. "Please!"

What? Martian zombies aren't usually so polite! Liz rushed downstairs and pulled the front door open. Jeff tumbled in.

"We've gotta hurry!" he gasped. "It's really late and I can't find Holly anywhere! She's not home. She's out there!" He pointed to downtown Grover's Mill.

Liz stared at Jeff's face. It was all wrinkled up in a frown that Liz knew was Jeff's way of showing fear. "No time for a song, pal. Let's go!"

They ran out the door and down the street toward the center of town.

Jeff huffed to keep up. "I told my dad everything, and he said there was no such thing as zombies. Then he disappeared into his little room and I heard buzzing and beeping."

"We'll have to get into that room someday, Jeff," Liz said. "But for now, we need to run!"

They flew full speed to the end of Oak Lane, then up Birch Street. The shadows were getting longer, spookier. The sun was dipping behind the purple mountains to the west.

Liz turned to Jeff. She was trembling all over. "Jeff, a zombie attacked me in my house."

"Did he get your forehead?" Jeff asked.

"No," she said. "I'm okay. But I don't really know why he didn't get me. I guess I fainted. When I woke up, he was gone."

"Maybe Martian zombies are picky about what they eat." Jeff turned the corner toward Main Street. "Maybe they like their brains weird or something."

"Then Grover's Mill will be All-You-Can-Eat!" Suddenly, Liz stopped running. The scene before her was a nightmare.

Hundreds of zombie surf commandos from Mars were pouring out from every alley, lane, road, and street in Grover's Mill. They charged over every square inch of downtown!

Stomping, scraping, shuffling, groaning, moaning, and whining filled the air.

Everyone ran wildly to escape. They cried out in terror! They tried to run! But everywhere ugly zombies were tapping foreheads!

Rob and Bob, the Double Dunk twins shrieked and scrambled inside the Donut Den.

Principal Bell, still trailing a slip of bathroom tissue from his sandal, tumbled away from a band of growling attackers.

"Whoa!" shouted Jeff, "I'm going to make like a tree and — leave!" He took off down the street.

"No!" shouted Liz. She grabbed his arm, zigzagged through a line of parked cars, and ducked into the registration gill of the fish-shaped Baits Motel. "Jeff, I'm going to say something to you that they say in every junky movie I've ever seen."

"Like what? We're going to die here?" said Jeff, peering from the gill to see old Mr. Usher flinging pancakes at zombies charging his restaurant.

"No." Liz shook her head. She took a breath. Terror stampeded through her ka-thumping heart as she spoke. "Jeff, it's all up to us!"

"Yeah, right," he snorted, almost laughing. Then he looked into her face. "You're serious! You mean it? *Us?*"

Liz pointed at the incredible scene before them. Zombies shuffled over every inch of Grover's Mill. People were screaming and

running. "The zombies want brains. They'll stop at nothing."

Jeff paused for a moment. "I guess you're right. We can't let them take over."

"Oh, it wouldn't be so bad," a voice droned behind them. "Why not let the zombies get you?"

Jeff whirled around and stared into the shadows of the Baits Motel. He grabbed Liz with one hand while he cupped his mouth with the other, trying to keep his breakfast in. All that mustard.

If he had a third hand, he would have pointed it at what he saw. He didn't, so he just nodded.

Liz turned. "No!" she gasped.

"Become one of us!" the voice groaned from the shadows.

Liz felt sick when she saw the eyes roll around so dull and blank.

The figure stretched out its arms and shuffled toward them, leaving little gray sneaker prints behind it on the floor.

"Holly!" Liz gasped. "You're a zombie!"

Kid Brains

Holly Vickers shuffled closer, her fingers pointing at the two wrinkling foreheads in front of her. "Mmmm. Brains!"

A shock of pain pierced Liz. Her best friend in the world had gone creepy. Liz felt even more alone. She stepped back. "Stop!" she shouted. "This is stupid! You're Holly Vickers. You're not a zombie! At least not yet."

Holly stopped and wobbled. Her skin wasn't flaky yet, but it was turning gray and the spot on her head was bigger. Her eyeballs were dry and staring. Her arms stuck out stiff in front of her.

The slapping and tapping of the zombie

bongo drums was like a war chant filling Liz's ears. She remembered the words of the creepy beach song.

Fresh brains are good for what ails us,
Until the mother ship sails us!

Suddenly — *JRIZZZZ!* — an idea sparked in Liz's mind. Everything fell into place like marbles on a Chinese checkers game. She brightened like a lightbulb in an oven when you click the switch.

"Yes!" she said.

"What is it?" asked Jeff.

Liz craned her neck and looked down the street. "The Donut says it's almost eight o'clock. We have to hurry!"

Jeff stared at her. "What? Are you hungry?"

"Yeah, for popcorn. We're going to the movies! Now grab Holly and follow me," Liz said.

Jeff pulled back. "No way. She's not gonna eat *my* brain!"

The screams from the street sounded horrible.

"Holly doesn't want your brain, Jeff. At least not yet. And if we act fast, she never will."

He frowned. "What's wrong with my brain?"

"Jeff!" cried Liz. "Work with me here!"

Jeff swallowed hard and grabbed Holly's outstretched arms. "Oh, all right, come on."

"O . . . kay . . ." zombie Holly droned.

The three kids crept along the sidewalk, keeping close to the buildings. Night was falling quickly. The streetlights cast eerie shadows on the pavement.

"Why are we going to the movies?" Jeff asked.

"I'm starting to figure some things out," said Liz.

"Good, because I'm not," said Jeff, darting looks everywhere.

"Okay," Liz began. "Martians are flying by Grover's Mill, right? I mean, of course

they are. This is the UFO landing center of the universe. Anyway, they see the flood-lights from last week's movie. But something happens and they crash in Lake Lake."

"Martians crash," Jeff repeated thoughtfully. "Uh-huh, go on."

"But the minute they hit Earth's atmosphere — *blam!* — they start flaking apart! And they attack us because they're way hungry and need brains to keep them from drying out."

"Wow, when you say it, it sounds so simple!" Jeff said.

"But I think I know how to get rid of them," said Liz.

"You do?" asked Jeff.

Liz nodded, took a deep breath, and told Jeff her amazing plan. Every single detail about how it was supposed to work. When she was done, she said, "And that's how we do it!"

"That's it?" Jeff screwed up his face as if he were sucking on one of those limes she sang about. "But you'd need incredible split-second timing. No way. It's too weird. Too dumb. Too impossible!"

Liz smiled. "Sure — anywhere else in the universe. But this is — "

"The Weird Zone?" Jeff offered.

"Exactly!" Liz gazed up and down the street. She had her eye on the Plan Nine Drive-in. It was almost eight o'clock. She didn't want to miss that movie. "This alley behind us looks safe. If we follow the back street, then shoot straight for the gates of the Drive-in, we should make it."

They started down the alley. The glow from a yellow streetlight cast deep shadows on the walls. A truck was parked at the end of the alley.

"Ohhhh!" A groan.

Something moved in the shadows.

"Who — who — who's there?" Jeff asked.

A large shape emerged into the yellow glow of the streetlight.

"Principal Bell!" cried Liz, running up to him. "Boy are we glad to see you. We need to get to the Drive-in, fast! Can you help us find a way to — "

But, Principal Bell wasn't the same somehow.

His skin was as gray as the linoleum in the main hallway of school, only it wasn't shiny like that floor. It was dusty like the floor gets when Mr. Sweeney the janitor puts that green stuff down after a kid throws up.

The look from Mr. Bell's eyes was dead. There was a big dark spot on his forehead. And as he lurched forward, he tilted from side to side like a kid on a bike with training wheels.

"Um . . . Principal Bell?"

"*Ohhhh!*" he groaned as he lunged for them.

"We're studying very hard!" Liz blurted out.

Mr. Bell stopped.

"Um . . . yeah!" Jeff added. "We're sticking to the summer reading program. Ten books so far. Fat ones!"

"Books," the man droned. "Summer reading."

This seemed to make a difference to the zombie Mr. Bell. "Gooood," he groaned, nodding. He pointed to the end of the alley. "Truck. Drive."

"Hurray!" shouted Jeff. "He's like Holly. He's not a total zombie yet. He's still human!"

"Well, let's not get carried away," Liz whispered under her breath.

A moment later, Principal Bell was at the wheel of the old truck. Liz, Jeff, and Holly were crammed into the seat beside him.

"To the end of the street!" shouted Liz.

"Street," Mr. Bell droned, jamming his socked and sandaled half-zombie foot to the floor.

They rounded the corner from the alley and ran right into the Martian commandos.

RRRRRRRRR! went the truck.

Beep! Beep! went the horn.

"Ohhhhh!" went the zombies.

Principal Bell cranked the wheel and spun the truck around as dozens of zombies charged.

A Martian lunged for the truck and grabbed the door. Mr. Bell veered sharply again, and the Martian fell off. Well, most of him did. A flaky gray hand dangled from the door handle.

"They want us!" cried Jeff. "We've got the only living brains in a hundred miles that are good enough to eat."

Liz knew he was right. Kid brains *were* the best. It was all that reading for Mr. Bell's program. Mr. Bell — if he was ever Mr. Bell again — would be proud.

The zombies abandoned the truck and charged once again at the helpless townspeople.

Poor Zoners, thought Liz. Even they deserve to live! She glanced back at the giant donut. Two minutes left! And only the most impossible luck would keep her incredibly complicated plan from falling apart like day-old zombie skin!

KRRRRAACKKKK!

Principal Bell burst through the giant gates of the Drive-in and screeched to a stop at exactly one minute before eight. "Movie!" he droned.

Jeff jumped out and shut the iron gates.

Liz jumped out and opened them again.

"Hey," Jeff yelled back. "Close those! The ugly dudes will get in."

"That's the idea!" Liz called out.

Zombie Fighters!

Liz grabbed Holly and ran straight for the old wooden ticket booth just inside the gate. Holly's father, Mr. Vickers, was inside. He screamed when he saw his zombie daughter, then reached for his video camera. "Holly, don't move."

Jeff tumbled into the booth. "Mr. Vickers! We've got good news and bad news. The good news is you'll get a lot of people at your movie tonight. The bad news is — they're dead!"

The man beamed. "As long as they pay!"

Liz ran back out to the gates and looked with terror on the scene before her. Men, women, parents, old people, kids, cats, dogs, gerbils, hamsters — all running from the zombie commandos pointing at their foreheads.

Jeff stood next to Liz. "Your plan will work. I'm sure it will."

Then — it happened. Everything at once.

Bong! sounded the Double Dunk Donut.

Ssssss! went Usher's pancake pan.

"Eight o'clock!" Liz shouted.

THONKA-THONKA-THONKA!

A terrible tornado of noise roared over them!

"It's Mom!" yelled Jeff, waving to the black chopper as it roared by overhead. "Coming home from the shoe store right on time!"

As soon as they heard the horrible noise, all the people of Grover's Mill dropped instantly to the ground. They lay perfectly still, as if they were dead.

"Perfect!" yelped Liz. "Everybody drops

just like you said, Jeff! Now I hope it works!"

The zombies stopped in mid-shuffle. They looked at each other. Skin fell off. They looked at the people lying motionless on the ground. More skin fell off. They didn't know what to do. "Dead brains — no good — yuck!" one of the creatures snorted.

"Yes!" cried Liz. "Zombies don't like dead brains. Only living ones!"

With that, Liz sprang into action. "Mr. Vickers, you take Holly and, when I give the signal, you do the total gross-out, skin-crawling scare you talked about. Jeff, you wait in the ticket booth and close the gates behind the zombies."

Jeff frowned. "Should I make them pay?"

Mr. Vickers stroked his chin. "Well okay, half price for dead people."

"But first, we need to get them here!" Liz ran across the lot to the giant screen at the far end. She climbed up a metal ladder all

the way to the top. She stood high above everything.

"Lights, please," she called down.

FLINK! FLINK! Mr. Vickers switched on the huge floodlights and the air went white with crisscrossing lights, sending signals miles around that the movie was about to start!

Liz stood amid the lights and began swaying back and forth high above the town. *"Come!"* she sang.

Come and meet
The brainy head so sweet!
The tread of zombie feet
    Will bring you to —
    I'll sing you to —
a huge moist brain to eeeeeeeeeat!

The song caught the aliens' sagging ears. They began to sway in the streets. They followed Liz's haunting melody.

From every street, alley, sidewalk, and yard in Grover's Mill, they came, shuffling over the townspeople and into the Plan Nine Drive-in.

"Customers!" Mr. Vickers beamed, still holding his camera. "A full house!"

On! On came the zombies! They tramped toward the lights, toward the music.

Once the parking lot was fully packed with zombies, Jeff shut the gates behind them and jumped back into the ticket booth.

The night was ripped by a horrible noise. *Unnnngh! Slaaaah! Unnngh!*

Then came the frightful words: *"Blobbo, the Hideous Mutant Brainoid has come for you!"*

The zombies all twisted their flaky necks to see an enormous slimy green brainoid quivering next to the ticket booth!

Oozy liquid was dripping from its teeth.

Two black eyeballs glared down from a lobe.

The total gross-out, skin-crawling scare!

At once, the zombie leader pointed at Blobbo. "A hideous mutant brainoid is still

a BRAIN!" he gurgled. "And what a —
BIIIIGGG BRAIN!"

The zombies saw supper. Supper big
enough for all of them! They grunted. They
groaned. They whined. They charged the
ticket booth!

"Oh, no!" shouted Liz. "Jeff's in that
booth!"

12

Keeee-oooo!

Liz climbed down from the screen as fast as she could. She ran toward the booth.

She knew Jeff was trapped in there.

Maybe it was already too late.

"Got to help Jeff!" she cried.

Even Holly stumbled across the parking lot, muttering, "Help Jeff. Help Jeff."

Liz screeched around a squad of shuffling zombies and dived into the booth. In the dimly lit little room, Liz saw several zombies just inches from Jeff, their fingers stretching for his head.

Liz eased along the wall, keeping her eyes on the zombies. She watched Jeff and the creatures just looking at each other.

"Jeff," she whispered, "what are you doing?"

"Staring them down," he explained. "Waiting for them to blink. This is good. I'm winning!"

Liz shook her head. "Zombies don't blink, Jeff. They're already dead."

Jeff seemed to take a moment to think about that. He looked at the gray faces staring at him.

"Oh," he murmured.

"Oh," he murmured again.

Liz crept forward. "Get ready to blast out of here." She stepped into the light. The zombies shifted their gaze. Slowly, Liz lifted her bangs and showed her forehead. The creatures lunged toward her.

"Hey!" Jeff cried. "What's wrong with *my* brain?"

"Just run!" Liz yelled.

He ran. Liz ran, too. In a flash, the two kids leaped through the booth door and tumbled to the ground. When they got up, Blobbo the giant brainoid was nothing but a wet spot on the ground. Mr. Vickers was running across the parking lot with Holly in his arms.

"Uh-oh!" Jeff gasped. "The zombies want dessert!"

Liz ran over to the floodlights. "Quick, help me with these!" Jeff helped her arrange the large white lights to crisscross the black sky. "Now we wait. And we hope."

"And we die," muttered Jeff as the Martians moved in. "Better practice your zombie shuffle. Because in half a minute — "

Keeee — oooo — keeee — oooo!

An eerie sound filled the air. The sky was suddenly electric and the black night exploded to purple, green, aqua, and red.

Then, as Liz and Jeff watched, an enormous round ship descended from the sky.

It sparkled and streamed with thousands of lights whipping around in a gigantic circle.

That Word Again

"Out of towners!" gasped Liz, staring up at the giant shape moving over them. "It's the mother ship!"

It was an awesome moment. Larger than anything Liz had ever seen, even larger than Lake Lake, a huge flying saucer, glowing with blinking bright colors, hovered above the entire town.

"Wow!" cried Jeff. "It's beautiful!"

A wavy blue light came waterfalling down from the giant ship and covered all of them. The entire town of Grover's Mill was bathed in the piercing blue light.

"Nice effect," muttered Mr. Vickers, reaching for his camera.

"Wha — wha — what's going on?" said a voice.

Liz and Jeff whirled around to see Holly, pink and cheerful, staring up into the blue beam.

"You're back!" cried Jeff.

"What about my back?" Holly snapped.

Jeff smiled at Liz. She smiled, too.

The Martian zombies gathered themselves under the beam. It got brighter and brighter until Liz couldn't see anything. Then she heard shuffling and thumping, tapping and skipping.

An instant later, the Martians burst out of the blue light like a bunch of rowdy high schoolers.

They charged over to Liz and Jeff and Holly.

Wow! Blond lady Martians with long wavy hair and handsome men Martians with big chunks of slick black hair. Wow! Wow!

"Cool!" said Jeff, his mouth nearly dropping open onto his chest. "They aren't ugly anymore. They're like movie stars!"

One Martian pulled out the bongo drums and began tapping out a spooky but snappy rhythm.

Tap-tap! Tappa-tap! Tappa-tap-tap-tap!

The leader of the Martians stepped forward.

The kids edged backward.

Suddenly, the Martian flung one hand across his chest and extended the other in front of him.

He gazed into the distance and began to sing.

As we saucered by
We saw lights in the sky.
But crashed into your lake and saw stars.

"The floodlights from last week's movie!" said Liz. "I knew that's what brought them here."

"Rodeo Mummies," Mr. Vickers beamed. "One of my scariest features."

Hey, the surfing was great,
But now it's getting late,
And we're bound for the planet that's ours.
So we bid you farewell,
Being zombies was swell.
But now we're just commandos from Mars.
Oh, yes, we're Surf Commandos from Marrrrrrrrs!

Moments later, the waterfall of wavy blue light shone down again, and all the Martians waved politely and floated up into the ship.

Keeee — oooo — keeee — oooo!

In a flash they were gone.

"Wow," said Jeff. "Those guys really have style."

The rumbling sound of the giant flying saucer died away across the desert sky.

The night air grew cool and hushed.

"I really liked the blue beam," said Holly with a big smile. "Being a zombie was kind of strange."

Then, from out of the darkness of the night, a woman darted up to the three children. She was all dressed in a military uniform.

"Mom!" Jeff shouted.

"Your father said something about zombies?" she said.

"Take a look," said Jeff, pointing to the lights vanishing in the sky. "Zombies from Mars!"

The woman shook her head. "Zombies don't really exist, son. But if they did, be thankful they weren't from Pluto. Zombies from Pluto are the most vicious brain eaters in the galaxy!"

Liz looked at her. "How come you know so much about alien zombies, Mrs. Ryan?"

Mrs. Ryan frowned. "I . . . uh . . . talk to some interesting people, when I . . . uh . . .

sell shoes." She quickly backed away. "I've got to find a phone." A moment later she was gone.

"Hey!" said Jeff, huddling close to his friends. "Do you realize we just saved Grover's Mill! Pretty cool, huh?"

As they walked, Liz rolled the words over in her brain like a baker rolls dough. Saved Grover's Mill. Did she do the right thing?

She gazed out on the town. Double Dunk Donut Den. Usher's House of Pancakes. Lake Lake. A town full of Zoners.

Actually, she felt sort of proud of herself and her friends. And even relieved that things were back to . . . well . . . the way they usually are in The Weird Zone.

Holly looked up into the sky. "I'm glad they got to go home. They'll be a lot happier there."

Liz agreed. "Guys, it's been weird," she told her friends. "See you tomorrow." She turned onto Oak Lane.

In that instant she thought she saw something shiny flash across the sky toward the lake.

What was that about zombies from Pluto?

She shook her head, whispered a five-letter word beginning with *W*, slipped into her house, kissed her mother, and went to sleep.

Just another day in The Weird Zone.

Bong! went the donut clock.

Sssss! went the pancake pan.

THE WEIRD ZONE

#3

THE BEAST FROM BENEATH THE CAFETERIA!

Beware of the beast's really bad breath!

Hear the Crazy Donut Song!

Written and Directed by Tony Abbott

Catch the action!

Enter The Weird Zone!

At
W. Reid
Elementary
a weird thing can
happen at any moment.
And another weird thing just happened.
There's a beast beneath the cafeteria!
Did someone say food fight?
Is anyone safe from the hungry monster?

THE BEAST FROM BENEATH THE CAFETERIA!
Starring the kids of Grover's Mill: Liz Duffey, Holly Vickers,
Sean Vickers, Mike Mazur, and Jeff Ryan
Special Appearances by Principal Bell, Kramer Duffey,
Mortimer Mazur, and Gorga, the Monster Beast (as himself)
Written and Directed by Tony Abbott

Experience a million volts of pure weirdness!

Printed in amazing STOMP-O-VISION

SCHOLASTIC